P9-DFO-042

The EASTER BUNNY'S ASSISTANT

Jan Thomas

HARPER
An Imprint of HarperCollins*Publishers*

Hello. I am the
Easter bunny,
and this is my
assistant, Skunk.

Today we will show you how to make BEAUTIFUL Easter eggs!

STEP 1:
HARD-BOIL
THE EGGS

I'm so
EXCITED!

Uh . . .
Skunk, what is
that smell?

Oh, sorry. . . .
It happens when
I get **excited**.

Please try to control yourself.

STEP 2:
MAKE DYE
FOR THE
EGGS

Oh! Look at the **beautiful** color! It's so . . .

EXCITING!

Skunk!

Sorry.

STEP 3:
DECORATE THE EGGS WITH CRAYONS

Oh, I **LOVE** decorating eggs. It's so . . .

. . . so . . .

. . . pleasant.

AND EX

CITING!

STEP 4:
REMOVE SKUNK FROM ROOM (push if necessary)

Hey!

STEP 5:
DYE THE
EGGS

knock
knock

Now you have **BEAUTIFUL** Easter eggs!

knock
knock
knock

Should I let him help me **hide** the eggs?

You sure?

STEP 1: HARD-BOIL THE EGGS

(Ask for an adult's help.)

Put eggs in a saucepan. Cover them with cold water. Bring to a boil, reduce heat, and simmer for 9 minutes.

STEP 2: MAKE DYE FOR THE EGGS

Combine 1 teaspoon food coloring with 2 teaspoons vinegar in a cup. Add water to the halfway point.

STEP 3: DECORATE THE EGGS WITH CRAYONS

Have fun!

STEP 4: LOOK TO SEE IF THERE IS A SKUNK IN THE ROOM

If there is . . . remove it!

STEP 5: DYE THE EGGS

Gently place the eggs in the dye. Let them sit for a bit, then remove.

Now you have **EXCITING** Easter eggs!

For Jule!

The Easter Bunny's Assistant

For information address HarperCollins Children's Books, a division of HarperCollins Publishers, 10 East 53rd Street, New York, NY 10022.
www.harpercollinschildrens.com

Library of Congress Cataloging-in-Publication Data is available.
Library of Congress catalog card number: 2011001885
ISBN 978-0-06-169286-4 (trade bdg.) — ISBN 978-0-06-169287-1 (lib. bdg.)

Typography by Rachel Zegar
12 13 14 15 16 SCP 10 9 8 7 6 5 4 3 2
❖
First Edition

When cooking, it is important to keep safety in mind. Children should always ask permission from an adult before cooking and should be supervised by an adult in the kitchen at all times. The publisher and author disclaim any liability from any injury that might result from the use, proper or improper, of the cooking instructions contained in this book.